# Little James' Big Adventures

## Tanzania

## Janine Iannelli

Illustrated by: Michelle Iannelli

To order additional copies of this book, contact:
Xlibris
844-714-8691
www.Xlibris.com
Orders@Xlibris.com

ISBN:   Softcover      978-1-6641-7871-7
        Hardcover      978-1-6641-7872-4
        EBook          978-1-6641-7870-0

Print information available on the last page

Rev. date: 07/13/2021

This book is dedicated to Petrena Schell; a beautiful, vibrant, and down to earth Youtuber who's videos on Tanzania were so amazing that I had to reach out to her about her experience living in this incredible country. Thank you so much for your consult, support and enthusiasm in writing this book. I also want to thank Kileli for looking over and approving this book. I always strive to depict each country accurately and respectfully and I appreciate both of your efforts in helping me achieve that.

Little James dreams of places far far away,
That he hopes to visit and see one day.
Most people take planes or even a boat,
But this little boy travels differently than most.

It's kind of a secret so sshh don't tell,
But Santa Clause made it with a magic Christmas spell!

The adventure begins late after James and Susie get tucked in.

Then James opens his eyes and wakes up Susie with a grin.

"Yipee!" Susie squeals, "Are we going somewhere tonight?"
James smiles and answers, "I think we just might!"

They place their hands on the globe and gaze at the world inside.
"Tanzania!" says James, "Is where we wish to ride!"

The floor starts to shake and the ground begins to rumble.
Then they're sucked into the floor where
they both begin to tumble!

"Wheeeeeee!!!

The weather is warm to hot year-round ranging from 14-20 degrees Celsius and 58-85 degrees Fahrenheit.

Suddenly it's still and they feel warmth on their skin.
They open their eyes, ready for the adventure to begin.

They stand in a lively marketplace with
people talking and yelling,
They start to walk around to see what everyone is selling.

"What part of Tanzania is this James? It sure seems fun!"
"We are in Arusha, and our journey has just begun!"

The market is plentiful, the food is fresh and bright,
People are smiling, something just feels right.

They see rows of fruits and veggies as they walk on by.
There is so much to choose from and so much to try!

"I am a little hungry," says Susie, "can we get some food?"
"Yes," says James, "but I'll order in Swahili so we're not rude."

"Habari," says James, "That means, hello."
Then he orders two Chips Mayaii to go.

"This smells amazing but what is Chips Mayaii?"
"It's a french fry omelet, it's yummy just try!"

Susie's eyes light up after she takes a big bite.
"Woah this is delicious, oh my James you were right!"

"Now let's go to Lake Manyara and see what is there."
James puts Susie's hands on the globe and poof they are there!

Over 400 bird species have been documented at Lake Manyara National Park including the pink flamingo during their continuous migration.

As soon as they arrive Susie is amazed!

There's a flock of pink flamingos, she stares lost in a daze.

"Woah, Susie check out the lions relaxing in those trees!"

"Wait Tree climbing lions? I've never heard of these."

Because of the heat in Africa Hippos spend most of their time in the water. They are great swimmers and can hold their breath for up to 5 minutes! When fully submerged their ears and nostrils fold shut to keep the water out.

Next, they see hippos, monkeys, and baboons!

Then James checks the time and says, "Oh no it's almost noon!"

He gets out the Globe and says, "It's time for a Safari!"

They land in the middle of nowhere,

then someone says, "Habari!"

There stands a young boy in colorful clothes,
"You seem lost, would you like help from someone who knows?"

"Actually yes," says James, "I think that we do!"
"My name is Kileli, and I'm happy to help you."

"My people are the Maasai we've lived here for centuries."
"We're James and Susie and we love
making friends in new countries!"

The Elephant is the world's largest land mammal weighing up to 6.6 TONS (6,000 Kg).

Every year millions of animals travel 500 miles (805 km) across Tanzania and Kenya. It is called The Great Migration!

Rhinos can run extremely fast! They can run between 30 and 40mph (50-65km).

Giraffes are the tallest animal in the world, measuring around 16-18ft (5 m)

Together they see, elephants, lions and buffalos,
They see leopards, zebras, hyenas and rhinos!

They see warthogs and wildebeest and even giraffes,
They see antelopes, gazelles, and cheetahs running past!

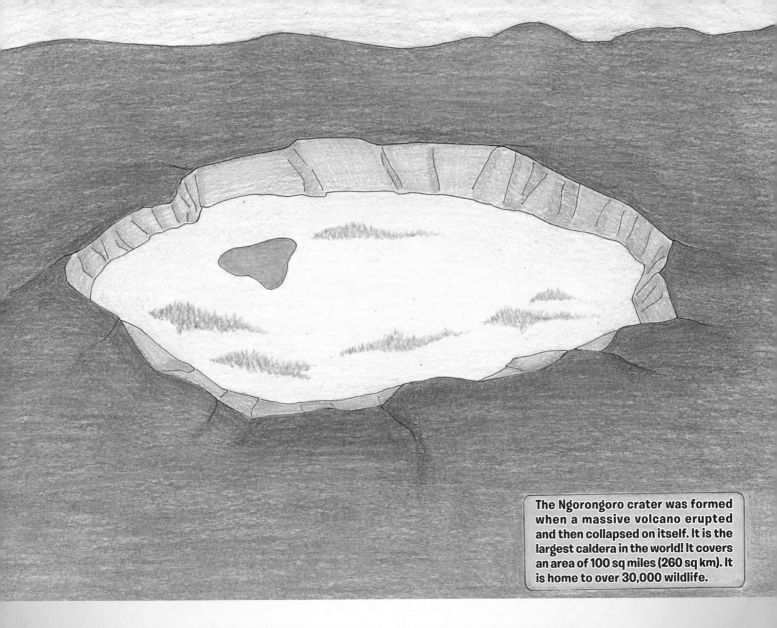

The Ngorongoro crater was formed when a massive volcano erupted and then collapsed on itself. It is the largest caldera in the world! It covers an area of 100 sq miles (260 sq km). It is home to over 30,000 wildlife.

Then Kileli shows them the Ngorongoro crater,
James and Susie gasp, "There is nothing greater!"
"It used to be a volcano, it erupted and then collapsed!
Now it's a world heritage site, and that is a fact!"

You two can come back to my boma if you like?
It isn't too far, it's just a small hike.

You can see how the Maasai live and eat.
"Wow thank you," says James, "that sounds really neat."

They go to his boma, which is a small community,
They all work together to live there in unity.

They build houses of mud, and live off the land,
They have lots of cows and the women's jewelry is grand!

They love to dance, and are friendly and welcoming,
They live deep in the bush, far away from everything.

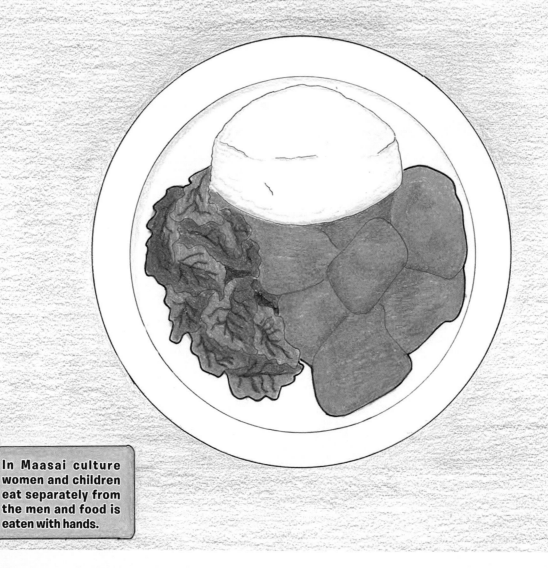

In Maasai culture women and children eat separately from the men and food is eaten with hands.

They make James and Susie something to eat,
It's a cornmeal dish called Ugali, and it's a real treat.

"Asante sana," says James, which means thank you very much.
You have all been so generous and Susie and I are so touched.

Friend in Swahili is Rafiki

This country is amazing, says Susie, "It has so many things!"
"Next you should go to Moshi says, Kileli
and see the hot springs!"
They say their goodbyes to their newfound friends,
They have lots more to see before the trip ends.

They place their hands on the globe and together say, "Moshi."
And they fall into a hot spring, it's both refreshing and toasty.
The water is clear and warm and surrounded by trees,
They relax and then notice tiny fish
swimming around their knees.
The fish kiss their feet, "It tickles!" Susie laughs,
"I think I can easily say this is my all-time favorite bath!"

Next James and Susie admire a massive waterfall,
"Wow," says James, "This country has it all!

And before we leave Moshi you know where we must go?"
"I do James I do, to Mount Kilimanjaro!!!"

Mt. Kilimanjaro is not just the tallest mountain in Africa but it is the tallest free-standing mountain in the world! It is also a dormant volcano with three volcanic cones.

They stare up at the giant Volcano, feeling oh so very small,
Out of all the mountains in Africa, Mt.
Kilimanjaro is taller than them all!

It's time to go now Susie, there's no more time to roam,
They place their hands on the globe and say,
"home sweet home!"

The ground splits open, James and Susie hold hands,
They close their eyes tightly and suddenly they land.

They land in their room and hop in their beds.
Too tired to talk, they just rest their heads.

James and Susie smile as they both fall asleep,
Happy to be home and with lovely memories to keep.

# Map of Tanzania

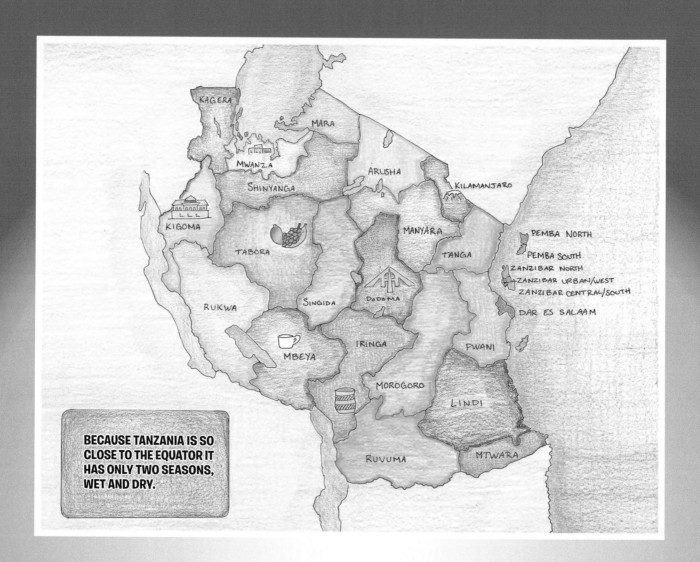

Find out where little James' magic snow globe takes him next!

Littlejamesbooks.com

Follow me on Instagram! @Janinelannelliauthor

Printed in the United States
by Baker & Taylor Publisher Services